For my parents, George and Shirley A. H. Bertrand — L. B.

For my grandmother, Janet G. Travell, M.D. — J. S.

With gratitude to Hans Teensma — L. B. and J. S.

One Day, Two Dragons

Story by Lynne Bertrand ☾ Pictures by Janet Street

Clarkson Potter/Publishers
New York

One day, two dragons caught a cab to Three Bug Street,

the address of General Dragon Central Hospital.

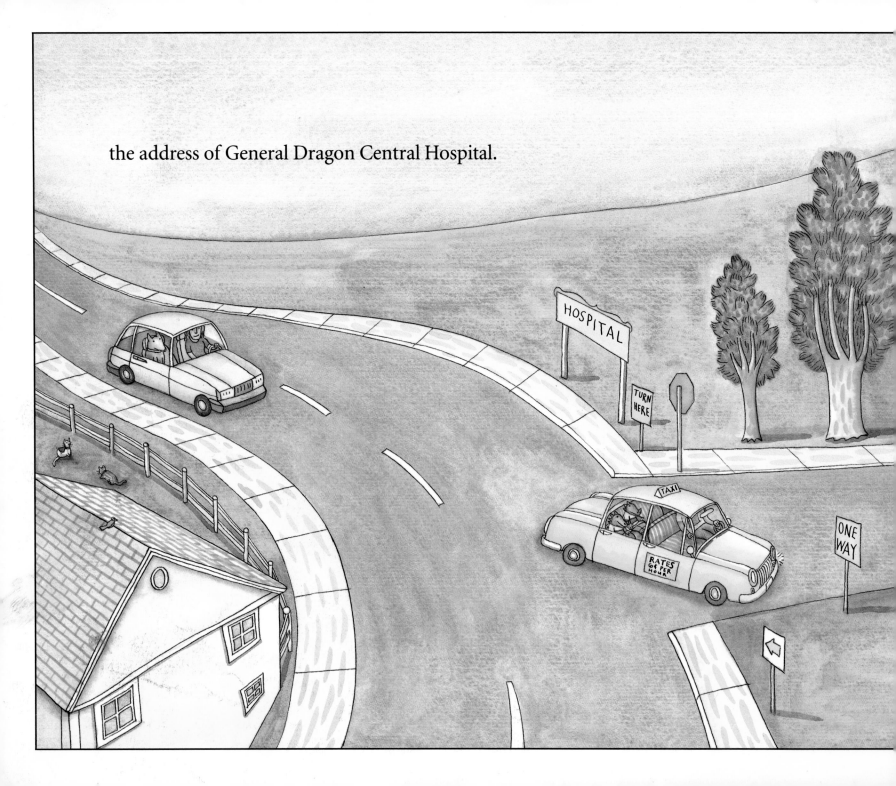

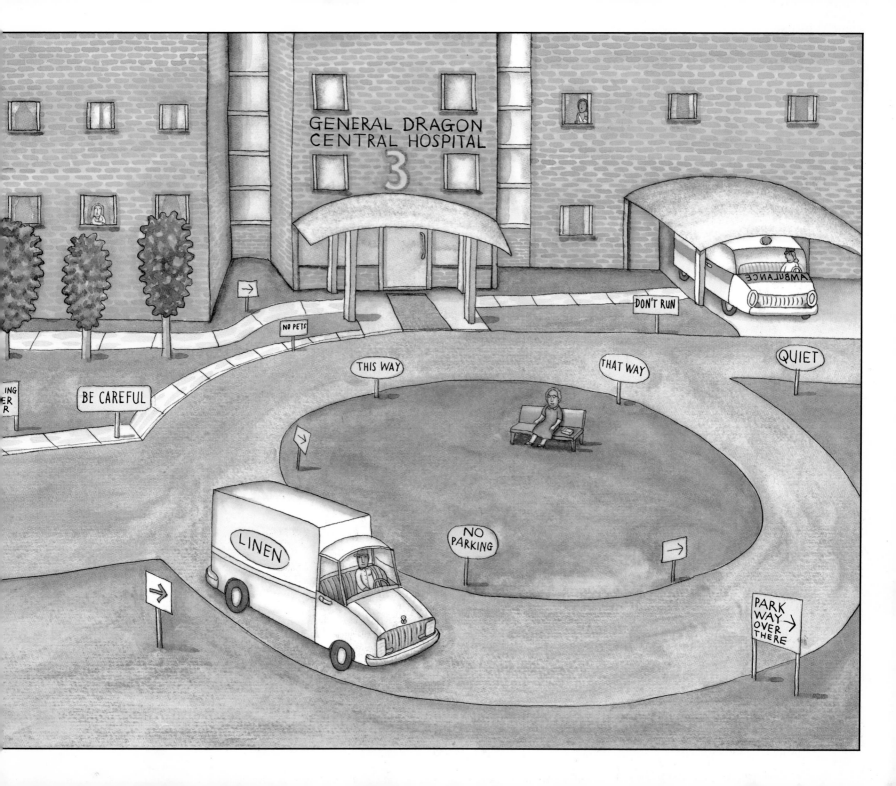

They needed to get four vaccinations, which, as you probably already know, are also called shots.

The shots were for measles,

mumps,

scale rot,

and morning breath —

illnesses that dragons can get if they're not careful.

Their appointment was for five o'clock.

The dragons were not excited about this. In fact, they were six minutes late on purpose, hoping the doctor would forget.

Seven chairs in the waiting room were empty and the dragons took
the seats closest to the door. They tried reading some magazines,
but couldn't concentrate. They read about eight words and stopped.

The receptionist at the front desk looked at least nine feet tall. She noticed that the dragons were staring at her, so she struck up a conversation. "I love getting shots," she said. "I get as many as I can, sometimes ten at a time."

"WHY?" asked the dragons, shocked. (Just then they also happened to notice that her fingernails were about eleven inches long.)

"I think shots tickle," she said. "All I can do the whole time is laugh. Afterward, when the nurse tries to give me a box filled with a dozen lollipops, I turn it down because I don't like candy." (As you probably know, a dozen is the same thing as twelve, which is a fair number of lollipops.)

"You've got to be kidding!" said the dragons.

The receptionist could talk for thirteen years about shots that tickle, and they still wouldn't believe her. They were looking down the hallway, which was about fourteen miles long, and they could see the nurse coming for them.

"Well, maybe we've got to go home now,"
said the dragons.

"Wait!" yelled the nurse. "Come back!"

The receptionist picked up the dragons and helped them into the
doctor's office, which they noticed was room number fifteen.

They sat together on the cold, silver table.

"Hello, dragons," said the doctor, "how are you today?"

"Fine," they said.

"How's school?" he asked.

"Fine," they said.

He asked them about sixteen more questions before finally mentioning the shots. "Well, how about a couple of shots for your health?"

"Fine," they said.

But it wasn't fine.

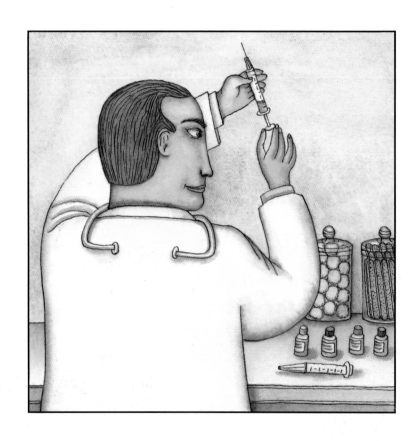

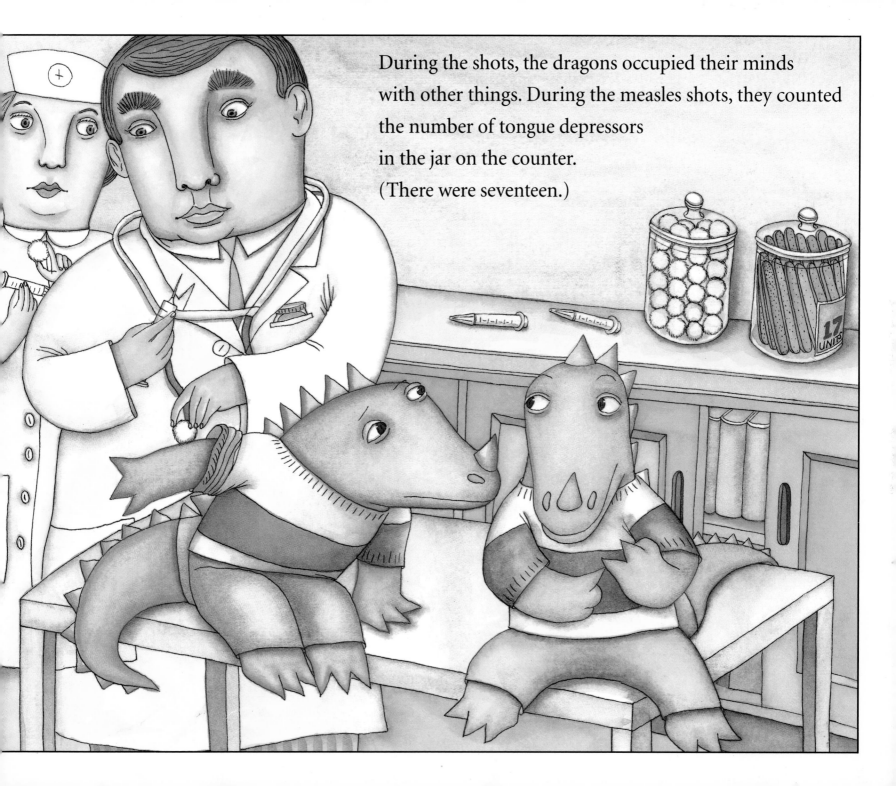

During the shots, the dragons occupied their minds with other things. During the measles shots, they counted the number of tongue depressors in the jar on the counter.
(There were seventeen.)

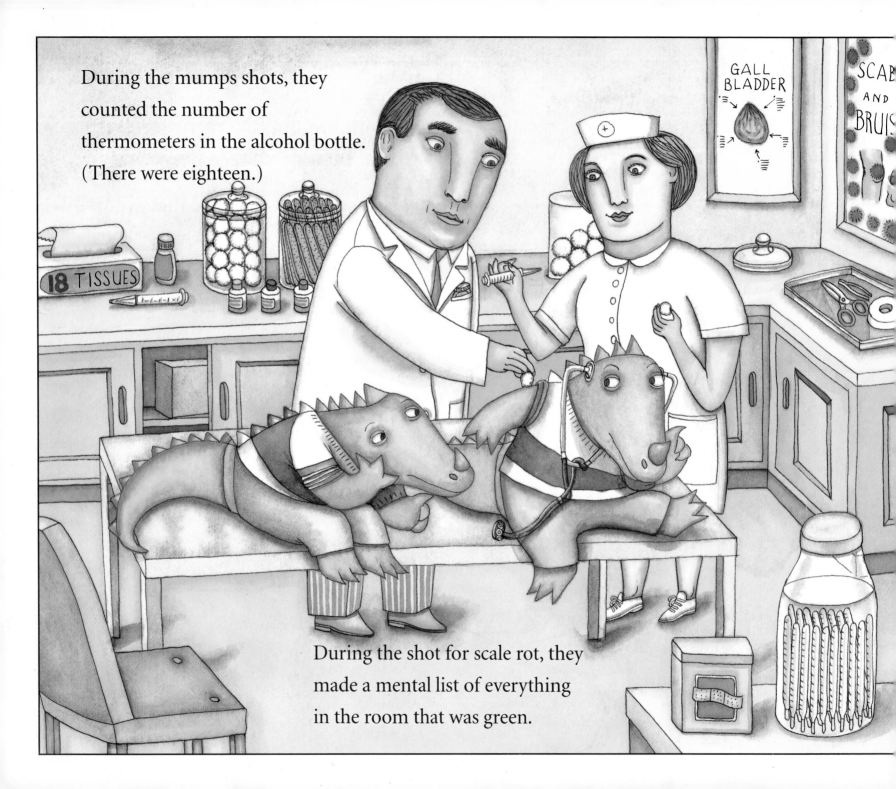

During the mumps shots, they counted the number of thermometers in the alcohol bottle. (There were eighteen.)

During the shot for scale rot, they made a mental list of everything in the room that was green.

GALL BLADDER

SCAB AND BRUIS

18 TISSUES

And during the morning-breath shot, they thought about their favorite thing, which is sneezing milk through their noses.

Afterward the doctor said they were fine dragons and the nurse stuck Band-Aids on their arms.

Well, the shots hadn't tickled, but they hadn't hurt very much either.
The dragons decided that being in the doctor's office was generally a lot
better than falling nineteen feet off the back porch and banging their heads.

In the end they did take the free lollipops offered at the front desk.

In fact you might not be surprised to know they took only the green ones,
which added up to twenty altogether.

Published by Clarkson N. Potter, Inc., 201 East 50th Street, New York, New York 10022. Member of the Crown Publishing Group.

CLARKSON N. POTTER, POTTER, and colophon are trademarks of Clarkson N. Potter, Inc.

Manufactured in Hong Kong.

Library of Congress Cataloging-in-Publication Data

Bertrand, Lynne.
One day, two dragons / story by Lynne Bertrand ; pictures by Janet Street.
p.   cm.
Summary: A counting book that relates what happens when two dragons go to the doctor's office at Three Bug Street to get four vaccinations.
[1. Counting.   2. Dragons—Fiction.   3. Medical care—Fiction.]
I. Street, Janet, ill.   II. Title.
PZ7.B463530n   1992
[E]—dc20

91-32743 CIP AC

ISBN 0-517-58411-5 (trade)
ISBN 0-517-58413-1 (GLB)
1 3 5 7 9 10 8 6 4 2
First Edition